5                                                    C2

F          Snyder, Zilpha
SNY           Keatley

           Black and blue magic

# Black
# and
# Blue
# Magic

ZILPHA KEATLEY SNYDER

# Black
# and
# Blue
# Magic

DRAWINGS BY GENE HOLTAN

ATHENEUM, NEW YORK

1975

# Especially for Douglas

Library of Congress catalog card number 66-12850
ISBN 0-689-30075-1
Published simultaneously in Canada by McClelland & Stewart Ltd.
Manufactured in the United States of America
By Halliday Lithograph Corporation
West Hanover, Massachusetts
Designed by David Rogers
First Printing February 1966
Second Printing June 1966
Third Printing September 1966
Fourth Printing November 1966
Fifth Printing February 1967
Sixth Printing September 1967
Seventh Printing August 1969
Eighth Printing August 1972
Ninth Printing January 1975

# Contents

Black
and
Blue
Magic

# Possibilities

On the very first morning of the summer vacation when Harry Houdini Marco was almost twelve years old, a pretty weird thing happened. Right at the time Harry didn't think too much about it, for some reason; maybe because he'd never been the kind of kid who went in for any sort of magic stuff. It wasn't until afterwards that he began to have second thoughts about what happened that day in the attic. But afterwards—considering the way the rest of the summer turned out—he decided he might as well believe there'd been something fishy about that first morning, too.

The day started out badly—about as bad as a first day of vacation possibly could. Harry's first chore was to mow the lawn in front of the boarding house, and it was right then that things started off on the wrong foot. Actually, Harry was feeling cheerful enough when he started, but, right smack dab in the middle of the mowing, a moving van pulled up in front of Pete Wilson's apartment a few doors down Kerry Street. Of course, Harry had known that the Wilsons were planning to move, but he *had* hoped it wouldn't be until the end of the summer. But no such luck. So there went Pete—not one of Harry's best friends but certainly the very last kid anywhere near Harry's age on the whole street. Moving to the suburbs, just like all the families in the neighborhood except the Marcos. Summer vacation suddenly began to look like a long lonely stretch of nothing.

Harry worked off a little bitterness by fiercely mowing down the last surviving column of tall green grass, and then he collapsed, feeling a lot like a mowed-down last survivor himself. But lying there in the sunshine—strangely warm weather for San Francisco in June—he began to feel just a bit better. The air around him was juicy with the damp green smell of cut grass, the sky was blue, and a whole three months of freedom stretched ahead. It looked as if something would almost have to happen.

He propped his heels up on the wheel of the lawn mower and began to consider the possibilities. Maybe somebody really interesting would move into Marco's Boarding House. Of course, there already was Mr. Brighton, except that he was so busy most of the time.

Even better, maybe Mike Wong would come to spend the whole summer with his grandparents at their grocery store on the corner. A whole summer of Mike would really liven things up.

Or it might even be possible that this year Mom would scrape together enough money for a vacation trip. That would be best of all. Every summer for years they'd talked about a trip, but every time it had fallen through. Of course, that wasn't Mom's fault. It takes a lot of money to go on a trip when, on top of all the other expenses, you have to pay someone to run a boarding house while you're gone.

But things had been better than usual at Marco's lately. There had been four steady boarders for quite a while now; and the two little rooms for temporary people had been rented fairly often by traveling salesmen. Yes, the Marcos just might make it this summer—if only the washing machine didn't go on the fritz again, or the furnace blow up, or some other dumb thing happen, as it always seemed to do just when they got a little ahead.

Thinking about all the things that could go wrong was bringing on a relapse of serious gloominess, when Mom came out on the veranda with a dust mop. "Well, if it isn't Hard-Working Harry," she said as she shook the mop over the railing. "I wondered what happened to you when I heard the mower stop half an hour ago. I was afraid you'd disappeared in a puff of smoke, but I see you only collapsed."

Mom hitched herself up onto the porch railing, pulled the old red kerchief off her head and ran her fingers through her curly brown hair. Sitting there on the veranda railing, swinging her legs, and sort of squinting from the sunshine on her face, she almost looked like a—well, like a girl, or something. Harry frowned. As a rule, he never thought much about how Mom looked. But now, he wished she'd get down off the railing and quit wrinkling up her nose that way. After all, a woman with an almost grown-up son—twelve years old in October—oughtn't to go around looking like a teenager, for Pete Squeaks!

After a minute or two, Mom slid down off the railing and started tying the kerchief over her hair. "I can't really blame you," she said. "That sun feels marvelous, after all the fog. But there is a lot to be done. When you finish recuperating from mowing that vast expanse of lawn, there are still the wastebaskets and the garbage, and that broken chair should go up to the attic till I can find the time to fix it. Oh yes, and Miss Thurgood wants you to go to the drugstore for her." Mom looked up at the sunny sky, sighed, and took her dust mop back inside the dark old house.

Harry sat up and scratched his ankles slowly, while he gave his mushy muscles a chance to get used to the idea of getting back to work. That part about the "vast expanse of lawn" had been kidding, of course. Mom was like that; kidding him into getting back to work instead of bawling him out the way some mothers would have done. Actually the lawn was so little that Harry was always scraping himself on something when he tried to turn the mower around to head back the other way.

Really, it was pretty silly to bother with such a dinky patch of grass. Harry had told Mom so more than once. But Mom said it was the only bit of green left on the block, and besides she could remember when she used to play games there when she was a little girl. Of course, things had been different then, and the lawn had been much bigger.

A lot of things had been different back in the old days when Mom was a girl. She had been Lorna Bainbridge before she was married, and the house had been Bainbridge Place, instead of Marco's Boarding House. There'd been lots of big old houses on the block then, and lawns and trees too. But times had changed, and where the big side yard had been, there was now a two-story cement building, squeezed in between Marco's and Wong's Grocery. Where Mom had once played tag on a green lawn, Jason's Cleaners steamed and hissed on the ground floor, and upstairs, Madelaine's School of Ballet tinkled and thumped.

Mr. Jason, the cleaner, wasn't much of a neighbor. He lived some place else, and at his shop he only worked, with no time for visiting. Madelaine was a little more interesting. She was a phony French lady from Chicago, and she lived right there in a little room at the back of the studio. Her ponytail was long and straight and skinny, and so was the rest of her. She looked even more so because of the things she wore—long underwear in bright colors. Mom said the underwear things were called leotards; and Mr. Brighton, who had lots of funny sayings, said that Madelaine had a shape like a yard of pump-water.

Anyway, even before Mom was born, the depression had started things changing, and now all but two of the big old homes were gone: Marco's, and the house right next door where the Furdells lived. And even the Furdells' house could hardly be counted, because a big brick and plaster building had been stuck right on the front of it, where Mrs. Olive Furdell made her candy and sold it.

Harry had scratched both ankles thoroughly, and retied one shoe, since he had first thought about getting up off the grass. There didn't seem to be anything else that needed doing, so he pulled himself together and stood up. The lawn mower, groaning and growling behind him as he pulled it slowly around back to put it away, seemed like an echo of his state of mind.

Usually Harry disliked the job of emptying the garbage and all the wastepaper baskets for the big boarding house, but today he was so busy brooding over his lack of prospects for the summer that he hardly noticed. But the next job, carrying a heavy rocking chair up three flights of stairs to the attic, was hard enough work to force him to give it his full attention. Even with his mind on his work, Harry managed to whack himself on the shins several times and trip himself once, when one of the rockers got stuck between two balusters on the staircase. Harry was too used to that sort of thing to get excited over it, but it did deepen his gloom a little.

Once inside the small fourth-floor attic, Harry cleared a space for the broken chair and then looked around for a place to catch his breath for a minute. A fat round of rolled-up rug looked fairly comfortable, and he collapsed on it on his stomach like a panther lying along a limb of a tree. It was while he was lying there in the warm, dimly lit attic, that the weird thing started happening.

He'd been lying there for a while with his chin on his hands, when his glance happened to wander into a dark corner—and he almost fell right off the rug. There, only a few feet away, a strange, white face was staring at him over the top of a marble-topped washstand. Harry's heart had time for only a couple of fancy beats

before he realized what it really was that he was seeing. Someone had put one of Dad's posters of the old Swami behind the washstand so that just the face stuck out over the top. Harry hadn't actually been frightened, but he couldn't help grinning a little in relief.

Now that he knew what it was, Harry remembered seeing the poster before. It was a phony-looking, old-fashioned picture of the Swami in fancy oriental robes and huge red turban. There were some big black letters across his middle that said THE GREAT SWAMI, but those were now out of sight behind the washstand. All that you could see was the pale wrinkled face, faded and dusty; and two huge dark eyes that for some reason seemed as bright as ever, so that they seemed to blaze out at you from the dim corner.

The poster had belonged to Dad way back when he was a boy. Even way back then Dad had planned on a career as a magician, and the old Swami, along with Harry Houdini and all the other famous magicians, had been his idols. Dad had turned out to be a magician all right, and when Harry was born Dad had named him after Harry Houdini—which at least was better than being named after the Swami—and Harry was supposed to grow up to be the greatest magician of all. Only, for some reason, Harry had never been able to fit himself into Dad's plans.

Harry was just lying there thinking about things like that, and wondering how he happened to turn out to be such an unmagical type, when all at once the Swami winked one of his big black eyes. For the next few seconds Harry was too astonished to think about anything, and before he could get his wits about him, the poster face smiled, with a hundred little rearrangements of wrinkles and a gleam of white teeth. A cracked and creaky voice that Harry remembered hearing once before said, "Remarkable weather we're having, isn't it?"

It was the usual kind of thing for people to say when it was warm in San Francisco in the summertime, but it was pretty unusual for a poster to say it. Harry had a little trouble getting his voice started when he said, "Yes, sir. Yes, it is."

The poster face turned a bit and seemed to sniff the air. "Invigorating," the creaky voice went on. "The air is absolutely heavy with possibilities. Don't you agree?"

"Well, I . . . that is . . . I guess I hadn't noticed," Harry managed to say.

The Swami's painted eyes focused sharply on Harry and he frowned. "Oh, but you must," he said sharply.

"You can't afford not to notice. Possibilities are easily missed. Possibilities are . . ."

Just about then Harry's chin slipped off his hands with a jerk, he blinked, and the poster face was suddenly stiff and silent above the marble top of the washstand. Without taking his eyes off the Swami's face for an instant, Harry got to a sitting position, and then slowly stood up. But the face in the dark corner stayed flat and faded even when Harry climbed over some stacked-up boxes, leaned across the washstand, and ran his fingers over the faded dusty surface.

Harry went back to the rolled-up rug and sat down to think. That's when he decided the whole thing must have been a dream. Of course, it had seemed awfully real and there *was* the fact that Harry almost never went to sleep in the daytime; but what other answer *could* there be. He stretched out on the rug again just to see how it would be for sleeping and, sure enough, it was soft and comfortable, and there was something very drowsy about the warm and slightly stuffy attic air.

Harry breathed a sigh of relief. That was it, of course. He'd gone to sleep looking at the poster and was dreaming until his chin slipping off his hands woke him up. Right at that moment, Harry was positive he'd found the answer, but just the same he couldn't help turning around quickly to grab a sneaking glance at the poster just before he went out the attic door.

He was still thinking about the dream as he went looking for Mom so as to get the money and prescription for Miss Thurgood's medicine. He found her on her knees scrubbing the tub in the second-floor bathroom.

The water splashing into the tub was making a lot of noise, so he just leaned against the door frame and waited, admiring the quick, efficient way Mom did the scrubbing. She did everything that way; fast, and with no waste motion. With a mother like that, and a father who had been a magician, with all the "hand is quicker than the eye" stuff, you'd think a guy would just naturally be well co-ordinated. You'd think he'd have extra good control of his hands and feet, instead of being the kind who usually couldn't make it to first base without falling all over himself. The kind who gets nicknamed things like Cement Hands, or Humpty Dumpty Harry.

Of course Mr. Brighton, who knew a lot about sports and things, said that Harry was big and strong, and once he quit growing so fast he'd probably stop being so clumsy. But it didn't look too hopeful. Here he was almost twelve years old, and things didn't seem to be improving very fast.

Mom sighed, sat back on her heels, and ran the back of her hand across her forehead. She turned off the water and stood up before she noticed Harry. "Well, hi!" she said. When she smiled, she didn't look so tired any more.

"Hi," Harry said. "I'm all through except going to the drugstore for Miss Thurgood."

"Oh, my goodness," Mom said, digging into her pocket for the money and prescription. "I'm glad you remembered. I was thinking about something else so hard I'd almost forgotten about it." As Harry started to leave, she went on. "I'm almost afraid to mention it, but you know what I've been thinking about? I've been wondering if maybe we'd finally be able to take that trip this summer. If we can just keep our steady boarders, and nothing expensive needs fixing, it looks as if we ought to be able to make it this time. At least for a week or two."

"Hey!" Harry said, forgetting all about everything else; gloomy moods and crazy dreams included, "That's great. Do you suppose we could go out in the country somewhere? Like on one of those farms or ranches that take boarders, sort of. What do they call those places?"

"I guess they're called guest ranches," Mom said. "We can look into it, I suppose, if you're sure that's what you want to do. I've heard those places are pretty expensive, but it won't hurt to inquire. Maybe we can find one that's not too expensive."

Harry made like a cowboy riding a horse and swinging a lasso over his head. "Yippee!" he yelled.

Mom laughed. "Now don't go getting your hopes up too high," she warned. "You know how quickly things can go wrong around here. We mustn't really count on it. But it does begin to look like a possibility."

Harry had started out the door but that turned him around with a jerk. "Did you say a . . . possibility?" he asked.

As Harry got out his old bike for the trip to the drugstore he was thinking it was too bad Mom happened to use that particular phrase. And just when he'd gotten the whole thing nicely settled in his mind, too. Of course, he was still positive that it had all been a dream. But you couldn't help wondering about things like— possibilities!

# The Medicine Mess

By the time Harry got to Brown's Drugs and Notions, he'd quit worrying about possibilities and was busy planning his two weeks on a guest ranch. In fact he was so busy he didn't even take time out to look over the selection of new funny books while he waited for Mr. Brown to fill the prescription.

Ordinarily, the funny book situation was the only good thing about having Miss Thurgood as a boarder. Mr. Brown was touchy about people who came in his store just to read the funny books. Sometimes he even made sarcastic comments in a loud voice about not running a lending library. But he didn't mind at all if an actual customer picked up something to browse through while he waited for a prescription to be filled. Miss Thurgood took just about enough medicine to keep Harry up-to-date on his favorite funny book characters.

But today he had other things to think about. For years Harry had wanted to live in the country. He had a favorite daydream about how he'd get a lot of money somehow—by winning a contest or getting a reward for some brave deed—and then he'd buy a ranch way out in the country. That way, he'd have the kind of life he wanted, and Mom wouldn't have to work so hard running a boarding house to make a living. Of course, two weeks wouldn't be as good as really living in the country, but it would be great while it lasted.

"Here you are, Harry," Mr. Brown said. "That will be three dollars and seventy-five cents." This time Miss Thurgood's medicine was red and syrupy and came in a great big bottle. It wouldn't fit in any of Harry's pockets so it would have to ride home in the bicycle basket. That meant that Harry had better get his mind off the country and put it very firmly on what he was doing. The last time he brought Miss Thurgood's medicine home in the bike basket something awful had happened. He'd forgotten the bottle of pills and ridden right over a curb with a big thump, and the bottle had flown out and smashed all over the street. At least it *had* been pills that time so Harry was able to find most of them and take them home in his pocket; but Miss Thurgood hadn't been very happy about her pills being "rolled around a dirty street and then stuffed into a *boy's* pocket." Miss Thurgood always said the word "boy" in a slightly disgusted tone of voice.

This time Harry rode very carefully and missed all the bumps, and the medicine was still all right when he came in the back door and put it on the kitchen table. Mom was working at the sink. They'd just started a very interesting discussion about how soon Mom was going to get around to writing letters to the guest ranch places, when Miss Thurgood's screechy voice called from upstairs.

"Oh dear," Mom said. "You'd better run up and take her medicine to her. She seems to be in a big hurry for it. She's called down three times to see if you were back from the drugstore."

Miss Thurgood was standing at the head of the stairs looking very impatient. When she saw Harry she said, "At last!" and shut her mouth firmly. When she felt like it, Miss Thurgood could close her mouth in a way that always made Harry expect to hear a clanking noise. Besides that, she could make her eyebrows come down almost to her nose. Harry never could understand how she could do that when her hair was pulled back so tight into the bun on the back of her head. Miss Thurgood's hairdo was one of the things Mr. Brighton had a saying about. He said with a hairdo like that one, you'd have to stand on your tiptoes to spit.

But Miss Thurgood was a good reliable boarder, and they were hard to come by, so it was important to keep her happy. Harry decided to run up the stairs to make it look as if he'd really been hurrying. It would have been a good idea, too, if anybody else had had it. Anybody except Humpty Harry—the World's Clumsiest Kid.

He was almost to the top of the stairs when all of a sudden one of his feet didn't get out of the way of the other one, and the next thing he knew his elbow hit the top stair with a crash that knocked the bottle of medicine right out of his hand. The next few minutes were almost too painful to talk about, in more ways than one.

Dinner time that night was pretty grim, too. Miss Thurgood kept having coughing spells behind a lace-trimmed handkerchief, and then explaining, in a gasping

sort of voice, how hard it was for her to keep going without her wonderful medicine.

Mr. Konkel looked concerned, and every time Miss Thurgood disappeared behind her handkerchief for another coughing spell, he would gaze at Harry accusingly. Mrs. Pusey and Mr. Brighton seemed to take it pretty calmly, though.

Mrs. Pusey was a quiet grandmotherly lady, with gray hair and sad eyes. She didn't talk very much, and it was hard to tell what she was thinking. You wouldn't know she was even interested in kids, except that once in a while she brought Harry a doughnut from the bakery shop where she worked.

On the other hand, Mr. Konkel was very interested

17

in kids—too interested. Mr. Konkel was the kind of person who seemed to feel that it was up to him personally to keep every kid he met from going to absolute rack and ruin. He had a million little lectures about what you should and shouldn't do, and he was always talking about juvenile delinquents and looking at Harry pointedly. He loved to tell little stories about what he did when he was a boy. Some people who do that are pretty interesting, but Mr. Konkel must have been just about the most boring kid who ever lived.

Anyway, Mr. Konkel listened very seriously to Miss Thurgood's story about how Harry had charged up the stairs and hurled the medicine bottle at her left ankle. According to Miss Thurgood it was only because she stepped aside so quickly, that the bottle missed her and smashed on the wall instead. Mr. Konkel kept looking at Harry and nodding his head as if it was just what he'd been expecting all along.

Mom was out in the kitchen when Miss Thurgood told the other boarders her version of the story. So it was up to Harry to set them all straight. But every time he got started Miss Thurgood drowned him out with another coughing fit. So, finally, he just gave up.

He was feeling pretty miserable until he glanced at Mr. Brighton. As soon as he caught Harry's eye, Mr. Brighton gave a wink and a grin that said he thought the whole thing was a big joke. And if you thought it over, it really was funny, except Miss Thurgood might move out; and if she did—there went her room-and-board money. And without Miss Thurgood's room-and-board money—there went the vacation trip.

# Mike Wong

The next morning Harry was on his way to Wong's Grocery to get two loaves of bread for Mom when he noticed the sunshine on the porch swing. The early morning sun was slanting onto the veranda making an inviting glow across the padded seat. Two days in a row of early morning sunshine right at the beginning of the vacation. It occurred to Harry right away that such an unusual circumstance ought not to be wasted.

He arranged himself on the warm pillows, being careful not to bump his sore elbow on the back of the swing. The elbow was pretty tender. After he was comfortably settled, and the swing had slowed to a gentle swaying, he twisted the arm around to get a better look. Sure enough, there was an ugly-looking purplish-red spot as big as a silver dollar. Harry examined it with a certain satisfaction. He was an authority on bruises, and this was going to be an impressive one. He thought briefly of showing it to Miss Thurgood to prove he really hadn't thrown the medicine at her on purpose, but on second thought he decided not to bother. He had a feeling that if Miss Thurgood wanted to believe something, there wasn't any use showing her evidence to the contrary.

In a mood of scientific curiosity, Harry decided to test his diagnosis. Lifting his right foot, he pulled up the leg of his jeans. Just as he expected, the bruise on his shin, although larger, didn't have nearly the color and quality of the elbow one. It hadn't hurt as much, either, although it had been just about as embarrassing. It had happened on the Sutter Street bus when he was hurrying to get off. He'd tripped over something—or maybe, over nothing, just as like as not. He'd staggered forward, grabbed a hand hold, spun around and wound up sort of sitting in a fat lady's lap. Afterwards, his shin had begun to hurt, although he couldn't remember bumping it on anything. He had a hunch, though, that the fat lady had kicked him. She'd looked as if she wanted to, anyway.

Examining your wounds is a good way to start feeling sorry for yourself, and it wasn't long before Harry had worked himself up into a very melancholy frame of mind. When you stopped to think it over, what did he have to be happy about? Here he was, probably the clumsiest kid in ten states, practically an orphan—at least, halfway one—living on a crummy old street where there was nothing but shops and stores and grownups. It was enough to give anybody the blues.

When Harry was really in the mood to feel sorry for himself he usually thought about his father. It wasn't just that is father was dead, either. It was sad, of course, that his father had died when Harry was only six years old, but that had been long ago, and time had dimmed the memory. Nowadays, Harry could feel even more miserable by thinking about what a disappointment he would be to Dad if he were still alive.

Harry could still remember just how Dad had looked; tall, and dark and slender—just right for a magician. There was a swift certainty about everything he did, and his hands could move so fast it made you dizzy trying to keep track of them. But most clearly of all, he could remember how Dad had planned and counted on Harry's becoming a great magician, too. Even when Harry was a little tiny kid, Dad used to try to teach him things: like how to handle cards and do tricks with handkerchiefs. Dad always said that Harry's clumsiness was only because he was so young, but Harry could tell he was disappointed.

And then, there had been the time that Dad took him to see the Great Swami. Harry grinned thinking about his crazy dream the day before in the attic. He had to admit he'd been a little scared there for a minute, but not nearly as scared as he'd been the time when he really met the Swami.

By the time Harry was born, the Great Swami was such an old man that he didn't do a stage act any more. But he'd once been famous for mind-reading and foretelling and Dad wanted the old Swami to tell Harry's future. Partly, Harry had been scared because the old man looked like a shriveled up old lizard in a turban, but mostly he'd been afraid of what the Swami might say. He just didn't know how Dad would take it if the Great Swami said that magic was always going to be a problem for Harry.

But strangely enough it had turned out all right.

The old man had stared at Harry a long time and then in a slow, splintery voice he'd said, "The boy has a rare gift, and his magic will be of a very special kind." Harry never had been sure what that meant, but it seemed to make Dad happy. He talked about it a lot and he always called it "The Prophecy." After that he made Harry work even harder with the cards and handkerchiefs.

It really makes a guy feel miserable to think about messing up a prophecy and being a disgrace to a name like Harry Houdini Marco. So, because he was in that sort of a mood, Harry thought about it some more, until he had worked himself into a really colossal case of the blues. He was just doing a quick rerun of his list of troubles to see if he'd forgotten anything, when a familiar voice said, "Hey!"

Harry's carefully constructed castle of gloom exploded as he lurched to his feet with a force that sent the swing thudding back against the wall. "Hey Mike!" he yelled.

Mike Wong had been one of Harry's best friends for years—but only during vacations. That was because Mike really lived in Berkeley. It was only when school was out that he came to spend a few days with his grandparents, who lived in an apartment over their store on the corner of Kerry Street.

Mike was almost exactly Harry's age and just about the same size. But that's where the likeness ended. The difference was that Mike Wong was just about the best athlete that Harry had ever known. Mike could run the fifty yard dash in six and a half seconds, he had a terrific batting eye, and he could pitch a ball that was almost impossible to hit—and right over the plate, too. And in kick ball, he kicked a low hard fly that whistled over fielders' heads like a bullet. He could do it time after time without one goof, and without asking for "bouncies" either.

Mike was standing on the veranda stairs, grinning up at Harry. There was a bat over his shoulder with a mitt stuck on the end of it, and he had a ball in his hand. "Want to go to the park and knock a ball around?" he said.

"Sure," Harry said. "Just a minute till I ask Mom." He was halfway through the door when he remembered about the loaves of bread. "Oops," he said. "Hey, I better run down to your store first. I was supposed to get some bread a long time ago and I sort of forgot about it. I think I'd better get it before I ask about the park, if you know what I mean."

Mike grinned. "Yeah, I know what you mean," he said.

Mike's grandfather, Mr. Williamson Wong, waited on Harry at the store. Mr. and Mrs. Wong were quiet gentle people who gave suckers to little kids and let customers who were having a bad time wait and wait to pay their bills. They'd helped Mom out more than once when the boarding house wasn't doing too well. Except, maybe, for Lee Furdell, they were just about Harry's favorite people on the block.

When Harry and Mike clattered into the kitchen with the bread, Mom was so glad to see Mike again that she didn't say much about how long it had taken Harry to get back. She said it was all right about the park and she even made them some sandwiches to take along.

The bus ride to the park was just about long enough to catch up on all the gossip since Easter, when they'd last seen each other. Harry knew a lot of good places in Golden Gate Park where there was room to bat a ball around, particularly on a weekday when it wasn't so crowded. They found a nice deserted stretch of lawn and had a good time practicing batting and pitching and catching. Harry did a little better than usual and it really made him feel encouraged.

Actually, it wasn't that Harry was so awful at sports; at times he did pretty well. It was more that he was so unreliable. Just when he'd been doing fine, he was sure to fall on his face—or flat on his back, like the time he'd stepped on a ball he was trying to kick. But he always tried, at least.

Once, a long time ago, Mike had said, "The thing about you, Harry, is you've got guts. You never chicken out, no matter how much you goof up."

That was one of the nicest things anybody had ever said about Harry. But that was the way Mike was. Even though he was so great at everything, he never gloated, like some hot-shot types. And he always said some little thing to make you feel better. Even if it was just, "Nice try," or "Tough luck."

That day at the park started out to be terrific. Late in the afternoon a bunch of big guys, about fourteen years old, let Harry and Mike join their game and it was great to watch their eyes bug out when they saw what Mike could do. And Harry wasn't so bad himself. He hit a couple of Mike's pitches and caught a sizzling line drive without even spraining a finger. It would have been a neat day except for one thing.

They were resting under a tree before starting off for home, when something happened that spoiled everything. They'd been talking about how great it was that summer vacation had started and Harry said, "Hey, why don't you see if you can spend a lot of time at your grandparents' this summer? Maybe a whole month or two. We could have a lot of fun. We could go to the zoo and Playland and come here to the park." He broke off noticing the funny expression on Mike's face.

"It sounds great," Mike said, "but I guess I can't. My dad's got a summer coaching job at this old camp up in the Sierras. Mom and I are going with him, and we'll be gone almost till school starts."

So there went one of Harry's best plans for the summer. Poof! Just like that—the way his Dad used to make a fish bowl disappear in a puff of smoke.

# Harry to the Rescue

On the way home from Golden Gate Park in the bus, Mike kept bringing up good things to talk about; like how the Giants were doing; and this spooky TV show, about a huge bloodshot eye that came down from Mars and crawled around like a spider. But Harry had a hard time keeping his mind on the conversation. He was feeling too disappointed—and jealous.

He kept thinking that some people sure were lucky. Mike's father was a high school coach in Oakland; so, no wonder Mike was so terrific at sports. And if that wasn't lucky enough, now Mike was going to get to spend a whole summer in the Sierras. Mike had tried to make it sound as if it weren't anything great so Harry wouldn't feel bad, but that didn't fool Harry. There'd probably be swimming and all sorts of other sports, and maybe even horseback riding every single day. Harry sighed.

Mike went on chattering away and Harry mostly just sat there staring straight ahead. They were in their favorite seat, at the very back of the bus, and there wasn't anyone else in the whole back part except one funny little man. Harry noticed the man because he had a dusty out-of-date look about him and his hair stuck out in a funny way around the brim of his hat. He kept fidgeting all the time and looking at a big old pocket watch. He'd hold up the watch and then glance out of the window, and then he'd look under the seat where there was a great big suitcase that stuck out into the aisle.

Harry was just thinking, rather bitterly, that he'd be sure to fall over that suitcase if it was still there when they got to Kerry Street, when, suddenly the little man leaped to his feet. The bus had pulled to a stop and some people were getting on at the front door. The man grabbed frantically at his suitcase and started to leave, but it was jammed under the seat so tightly that it didn't come loose. Then when it finally did come loose, it came so suddenly that the little man staggered backward. By the time he got going forward again the door was starting to close. The little guy lurched through and made it to the sidewalk, but the suitcase wasn't so lucky. In the rush, it hadn't gotten turned around endways so, of course, it got stuck in the door. When the suitcase stopped coming, the little man's feet flew up and he sat down quickly on the sidewalk. The bus doors finished shutting and as the bus moved slowly forward, the suitcase just slid down into the step well and stayed there.

Afterwards, Harry couldn't imagine what had gotten into him. It really wasn't any of his business. Maybe it was because he knew what it felt like. Having fallen out of and into so many things himself, he knew too darn well what it felt like. Anyway, he didn't wait to explain it to Mike, who hadn't seen the whole thing, or to tell the driver, who apparently hadn't noticed it at all. Instead he just leaped to his feet, pulled the stop cord, and started tugging the suitcase up out of the step well. It was jammed so tight that he didn't get it loose until the bus had almost reached the next stop.

As he started out the door Mike yelled, "Hey, where are you going?"

"I'm taking this suitcase back to the man who lost it," Harry called back. "Want to come along?"

Mike started to jump up, but then he sat back down again. "I can't," he said. "I haven't any more bus money."

As the bus pulled away, Harry shouted through the window, "So long. See you later—at the store!"

It wasn't until Harry had started back down the sidewalk, staggering a bit under the weight of the suitcase, that it occurred to him that he didn't have any more money for the bus fare either. As he struggled along, setting the suitcase down now and then to rest and change hands, he began to realize that he'd done a pretty stupid thing—as usual. What if the man had hailed a taxi, or caught another bus? It would be impossible to find him. Harry couldn't just go off and leave the suitcase and, just as certainly, he couldn't walk all the way home carrying it. And how would it sound if he tried to explain it to a policeman? "Oh-er, Mr. Policeman. Have you seen a little man in a funny hat? You see, I jumped off a bus with his suitcase and . . ." No, Harry decided, it would be better not to try to explain it to anyone, except as a last resort.

But the suitcase was unbelievably heavy, and Harry had just about decided that he'd reached the last-resort stage, when he saw the little man. He was sitting on a bus bench with his elbows on his knees and his chin in his hands, looking terribly tired and dejected. His face, which Harry really hadn't seen before, was as round and pink as the Gerber Baby, only with wrinkles. But there was no mistaking the old-fashioned hat, or the hair that stuck out in funny little tufts over his ears. He looked so mournful, sitting there staring at the ground, that you couldn't help feeling sorry for him.

He didn't even look up until Harry tapped him on the shoulder. "Excuse me, Mister," Harry said. "I think this suitcase belongs to you."

The man jumped, gasped, and the minute he saw the suitcase he grabbed it and sort of hugged it up onto his lap. "Yes, yes," he said, "my suitcase. It *is* my suitcase. It really is my suitcase! I felt quite sure I'd never see it again. Quite sure. And here it is back again. I don't know how to thank you, young man. Indeed I don't." The suitcase was so big that he had to stretch to look over the top of it, and he kept patting it as he talked, as if to make sure it was really there.

"I saw you lose it on the bus," Harry said. He didn't mention the part about getting stuck in the door and falling down, because he always preferred not to have it mentioned when he did that sort of thing. "So I grabbed it and jumped off the bus as soon as I could, and then I came back this way looking for you."

The little man looked astounded. "You did that?" he said. "You really did? My! My! How very clever of you—and how kind. You really don't know how I appreciate this. You can't imagine how important this case is to me, and how necessary it was for me to get it back before . . . Well, I can only tell you that I would have been in very serious trouble if it had been lost or if it had fallen into the wrong hands." The little man's shoulders twitched in an uncontrollable shudder and for a moment he seemed lost in thought. Not very pleasant thought either, judging by the pained expression on his face.

Then suddenly he seemed to pull himself together. "But that's neither here nor there," he said, crinkling his face into a smile that made him seem, more than ever, like a weather-beaten cherub. With a jerky little bounce, he hitched himself over on the bench to make room for Harry. "You must sit down and rest a moment. I know only too well how tiring it is for a rather small person to carry this heavy case."

Harry was in a hurry to get started for home, but he sat down for a moment to be polite. The stranger was still chattering away. "I am greatly indebted to you. You can't imagine what the loss of my case would have meant. I'm very much afraid it would have been the last straw—the Final Mistake, you might say."

"Final?" Harry asked. The word had such an unpleasant sound.

"Yes, in a sense. At the very least it would have greatly increased my troubles."

"Are you already in trouble, then?" Harry asked.

"Trouble?" The man gave a deep sigh, and his face, for a second, seemed to take on a depth Harry would have thought impossible a moment before. "Is it not trouble that I am a wanderer upon the face of the earth; that I have no place to call my own; that my back is tired and my feet ache; that I must find a place to stay in a new city every few days . . ."

It was at that point that Harry interrupted. He hadn't helped run a boarding house for almost six years for nothing. "Have you a place to stay in San Francisco?" he asked quickly.

"I stopped at a small hotel last night. But it was not particularly satisfactory. If it looks as if my business will keep me in the city for a while, I may have to look elsewhere."

"I know just the place for you," Harry said quickly, pulling out his wallet. He always carried a few of his mother's cards for just such occasions. "My mother runs a boarding house on Kerry Street. Nice and quiet and good home-cooking. A lot of traveling salesmen come back to our place every time they're in town."

The man stretched his arm up over the suitcase to take the card. It was a little dirty and beat up, but you could still see that it said:

MARCO'S BOARDING HOUSE

318 Kerry Street

Mrs. Lorna Marco, Proprietress

Quiet—Comfortable—Good Food

"You are a salesman, aren't you?" Harry asked.

The little man gave one of his big sighs. "Yes indeed," he said. "I am a salesman."

"I thought so," Harry said. "I can usually spot a traveling salesman right away, because we have so many of them stay with us. I don't know, though, if I would have guessed about you or not. That is, if we hadn't talked. But I do know something about what you're selling, I'll bet."

"You know what I'm selling?" The man clutched the suitcase against his chest. His eyes peering over the top rounded with horror and then flattened with indignation. "You opened it!" he accused. "What right had you to open my case? You must swear that you will not tell . . ."

"Gee Mister," Harry interrupted. "I didn't open your case. I was just starting to say I knew it sure was heavy, whatever it was. I was just making a joke."

After a moment the man relaxed and sighed with relief. "I see that you are telling the truth. Forgive me. This has been a very trying day and I am not myself." He reached in his pocket and pulled out the funny old watch. "I must be going now. I have an appointment with a possible customer. But I will remember what you have done for me."

From a pocket inside his coat, he brought something out and handed it to Harry. "May I present my card in return," he said. The card was thick and heavy, with a worn and yellowed look about it. The printing was so fancy and so covered with curlicues that it was hard to tell what it said. It wasn't until later, that Harry made out all the letters and decided that it said:

Tarzack Mazzeeck
Representative-at-Large
for the
A. A. Comus Co.

The little man was glancing nervously at his watch again. "I really must hurry along," he said. "But we shall meet again soon. I fear I shall never be able to repay sufficiently the favor you have done me."

"Oh, it wasn't anything," Harry said. "And it was

nice meeting you, Mr. . . . Mr. . . ." He looked down trying to make out the printing on the card in his hand.

"Mazzeeck," the man said. "Tarzack Mazzeeck. Forever at your service." He stood up bracing himself against the weight of the heavy suitcase.

"Well, good-by, Mr. Mazzeeck. Be seeing you."

As Harry started off on the long walk home, he kept thinking about the odd little man. There had been something so unusual about him that it almost seemed now as if he really didn't exist. Harry felt as if the whole thing could have been another silly dream—except of course, this time it hadn't. It *had* really happened and only a few minutes before, too.

Maybe the whole thing had something to do with the air being "heavy with possibilities," Harry thought—not seriously, of course, but just sort of fooling around with the idea. For instance, what if there was a possibility that the guy was a billionaire in disguise and the suitcase had been full of his most valuable business papers. Maybe tomorrow Harry would get a letter with a million dollars reward in it.

It was a great idea, but Harry knew it was a dumb one. For one thing, papers, no matter how valuable, couldn't have weighed that much. And besides, Harry couldn't help feeling that, if the little man really were in disguise, he was hiding something more than the fact that he was just a common billionaire.

# Hot Water and Hysterics

Harry walked and walked and walked—past dinner time and sundown and twilight. It was almost dark when his aching feet carried him through the gate and around to the back door of the boarding house. The front door was a few steps closer, but some of the guests were usually in the living room in the evenings; and in case Mom was mad, he'd just as soon give her a chance to bawl him out in the privacy of the kitchen. He was hoping that she wasn't too mad and wondering if she'd saved him any dinner, when he opened the back door and got the shock of his life.

Mom was sitting at the kitchen table with her head in her hands and she was *crying*. Mom never cried—not that Harry ever knew about, anyway. When she heard Harry, she raised her head and started to brush the tears away with the back of her hands.

Harry felt awful. "Hey Mom," he said. "Don't do that. I'm sorry I'm late. It really wasn't my fault."

Mom sniffed and smiled, but the smile wobbled and so did her voice. "Oh, it's not that," she said. "I knew what happened to you. Mike came over and told me. He said he thought you were out of money and would probably have to walk home. It wasn't that at all."

"Well, what was it then? What happened?"

"It was the water heater." Mom took out a handkerchief and blew her nose. "It was the water heater . . and Miss Thurgood," she added in a quavery voice that ended up in a sob and then, all of a sudden, turned into a giggle

Harry was alarmed. It was beginning to look as if Mom was cracking up, right before his eyes. But just about then, Mom quit giggling and started acting like a normal mother again.

"I'm sorry to act so silly, Harry," she said. "But you just can't imagine what's been going on here. Right after dinner I was sitting in the front room talking to Mrs. Pusey. Miss Thurgood had just gone upstairs to take her bath. You know how she is about her bath."

Harry knew Miss Thurgood's baths, all right. She always took them early because she liked to use lots of hot water and soak for a long time. Miss Thurgood's bath was another subject that Harry and Mr. Brighton made up jokes about. Mr. Brighton said he bet she was soaking herself in vinegar, because she was in training to become a pickle.

"Anyway," Mom went on, "all of a sudden she called from the bathroom and said there wasn't any hot water. I called back that I'd check the water heater. You know it hasn't been too reliable lately. When I got to the kitchen, I found the whole floor flooded. The water was about a half inch deep and getting deeper. It was only warm though, so the fire must have gone out some time before. I waded over to the pantry, and sure enough, the whole bottom was out of the water heater, rusted clear through. I knew the thing couldn't last much longer, but I had so hoped it would hold out until after our vacation trip. I was so mad about having to spend some of our trip money on a water heater, and so worried about the water getting out into the hall, that I forgot all about Miss Thurgood. I found the little wheels that shut off the water, and I was just getting out the mop and pail, when Miss Thurgood stormed through the door. She had on that long old wool bathrobe she wears, and she had her bath brush in one hand and her bar of soap in the other. She just had time to say, 'Mrs. Marco! *Where* is my hot water?' when she stepped in it and her feet slid out from under her."

Mom started to giggle again. "She looked so funny sitting there in the water, with her bath brush still in her hand like a scepter, or something, that I . . . it was awful of me, but I just couldn't help it . . . I started to laugh."

By now Harry was laughing, too. "But that wasn't all," Mom said between snorts and splutters. "I said something, too. I said, 'You're sitting in it.'" At that

Harry and Mom both broke down and laughed until they were weak.

After a while Mom sobered down and wiped her eyes. "It's really not so funny, though," she said. "Miss Thurgood has gone. She dripped right up to her room and packed a bag and left. She said she'd been insulted and that she'd send for the rest of her things tomorrow. So after she'd gone and I'd finished mopping up the floor, I sat down here and started thinking about how I'd ruined our chances for a trip, after I've been promising you one since you were seven. We might have managed a short trip, even with a new water heater to buy, but with Miss Thurgood's leaving . . ." Mom shook her head sadly.

"Look, Mom," Harry said. "Don't worry about it. I've got plenty of things to do this summer. As a matter of fact, a trip might interfere with some of my other plans." Of course, that was a big fat lie, if there ever was one; but Harry said it so convincingly, that for a moment he almost believed it himself. The realization that the last of his summer plans had fizzled was just beginning to take hold of him when Mr. Brighton came in.

The kitchen door swung open, and Mr. Brighton's head appeared. "Well," he said, "if it isn't Mr. Harry Marco in conference with his chief assistant." Mr. Brighton was always kidding Harry about running the boarding house. He made a big joke out of it most of the time, but once Harry had overheard him telling Mom what a great job she'd done raising Harry. Mr. Brighton had said it was unusual and refreshing to meet a kid who shouldered responsibility so cheerfully.

Mom had said, "I know. Sometimes I worry that it's too much responsibility. But when I started the boarding house I had so much to learn, and Harry just seemed to learn right along with me."

"That's what I get such a kick out of," Mr. Brighton said. "Sometimes I think he knows more about running a boarding house than you do."

So Harry knew what Mr. Brighton really meant by that sort of kidding. But right now, Mr. Brighton didn't say any more about Mr. Harry Marco's boarding house. He seemed to have something else on his mind. He pulled out a chair and sat down. "I was wondering if there's any coffee available down here," he said. Harry got a cup and Mom poured some coffee from the percolator that she always kept filled on the kitchen table. "But to tell the truth, I'm also just curious. A little while ago I looked out my door to see if Miss Thurgood had finished marinating in the bathroom, and I was just in time to see her come stomping out of her room all dressed up and carrying a suitcase. Is anything up?" He grinned at Harry. "You been throwing any more medicine bottles lately?"

"No," Mom said. "I'm afraid I'm the guilty party this time, and I'm awfully afraid she's gone for good." Mom got up to get Harry a plate of food she'd kept for him in the warming oven, and then she sat back down again and told the whole story over for Mr. Brighton. Mom and Harry got hysterical all over again, and when she finished the three of them just sat there and laughed like a bunch of idiots.

# The Marriage Plan

It was while the three of them, Harry and Mom and Mr. Brighton, were together there in the kitchen, that Harry started his Plan. It really wasn't a plan at first, just the ghost of an idea; but that night in his third-floor room, he thought about it some more.

Sitting cross-legged on the foot of his bed, he could look right out of the window and across the bay. He often sat there when he had something special to think about. Sometimes the fog drifted in from the Golden Gate and rose higher and higher, drowning the city noise and glare in cool gray mist.

Harry liked it up there on the third floor. It was just a tiny place that was supposed to be a servant's room; but it was separate and private, and its little gabled window had the best view in the house. If he leaned right out, he could even see part of the downtown sky line right on the other side of Madelaine's clothesline and T.V. antenna. It had been his own idea to give up his big bedroom on the second floor. That way, they could take an extra boarder and, besides, he liked the third floor best.

That night, as he enjoyed his own private view, his idea began to form into a real plan. There were a lot of little things from which the Plan grew. First, there had been the other day when it had occurred to him that Mom was pretty young looking, and sort of cute, too. Then tonight, there'd been the way they'd all laughed together around the kitchen table. And part of the Plan was, of course, because of Mr. Brighton and the way he was.

Mr. Brighton was just about the best boarder that Marco's had ever had. He was a big tall man with curly grayish hair. He had a great sense of humor and he liked to talk about interesting things, like sports and animals. In fact, Mr. Brighton owned a farm. Well, it wasn't exactly a farm, but it was a place in the country, up in Marin County. It was a big old farmhouse with a barn and a small pasture. Before his wife died, Mr. Brighton had lived there and commuted into the city every day, and they'd had horses and all sorts of other pets. The farm was rented now, but once when Mr. Brighton had to go there to see about fixing something, he'd taken Harry with him. It really was a neat place.

The farm was one of the most interesting things about Mr. Brighton, but besides that he had a swell job. He managed a sporting-goods store on Market Street— everything from skis to bowling balls. Harry sometimes dropped in there for a visit when he was downtown, and Mr. Brighton always took time out to be friendly and show him around.

In the kitchen, Harry had just happened to think it was too bad that Mr. Brighton and his wife hadn't had any children, because he would have been a neat father. And that thought led to some others.

Mom had had some boy friends in the years since Dad died. Even Mr. Konkel had taken her to the movies once or twice, and bought her candy and stuff like that. But Harry could tell that Mom didn't like any of them very much. Particularly Mr. Konkel.

He'd never really thought about Mom's ever marrying anybody—or if it had occurred to him, he hadn't much liked the idea. But if you gave it some fair and unprejudiced consideration, you had to admit that having a stepfather might not be so bad after all. For one thing, Mom wouldn't have to work so hard, and for another, Mr. Brighton would be almost sure to want to move back out to his farm if he had a family to help him take care of it.

The more he thought about it, the more Harry liked the Plan. There were a few problems, though. The main one was that the idea didn't seem to have occurred to Mom or Mr. Brighton. Having been around grownups so much, Harry thought he knew the symptoms. Like the time Miss Dutton, who lived in the east room for about a year, had married Mr. Jenkins, who stayed at Marco's once a month, when he was in the city selling stuff to beauty shops. After they got married Mr. Jenkins didn't come any more, because Miss Dutton made him stop traveling.

Anyway, it always started out the same, with lots of silly compliments and staring at each other. Then came whispering and holding hands and giving presents. As far as he could tell, Mom and Mr. Brighton didn't have a single symptom.

Mr. Brighton always seemed friendly enough where Mom was concerned. Sometimes he even offered to help her out with heavy jobs around the house. But Harry wasn't sure you could count that. It wasn't a sure sign at least, like whispering or holding hands.

That night in his room, Harry got as far as deciding that he was going to have to do something himself. That is, he was going to have to find a way to get Mom and Mr. Brighton to really notice each other. That part of the Plan was easy to see. The hard part was figuring out how he was going to do it. He finally went to sleep thinking that maybe Lee Furdell would have some ideas.

The next morning, right after his regular chores were done, Harry went next door to the candy store, looking for Lee. But this morning, Mrs. Furdell was behind the counter so Harry didn't go in. People were always looking for Lee Furdell. Everyone in the neighborhood who needed advice or sympathy, or even just a free taste of candy, went looking for him. Nobody ever looked for Olive Furdell, and if you found her by mistake you knew better than to ask her for anything; even a little piece of information, like where her husband was that morning. You just went on looking.

The candy store filled the entire front yard of the Furdell place, right up to the sidewalk, but a tiny narrow alley led around the side of the gingerbready old house to the back yard. Lee was in the back yard hanging out the wash. When he saw Harry, he stopped right away and sat down on the back steps to have a talk. Lee was like that.

"Well, sit down Harry," he said, patting a place beside him on the stair. "Let's catch up on the boarding house gossip. You haven't been to see me for so long. I'm afraid I'm all out of date."

Mr. Furdell was a small man with limp hair and big soft eyes, like some sort of woods animal. He didn't look very interesting until you got to know him. But everyone who knew him agreed that he was one of the greatest guys in the neighborhood. That is, everyone except his wife, maybe.

Ever since Harry first came to Kerry Street, he had been taking his broken toys, his kites that wouldn't fly, and his problems to Lee—that was what everybody called him, even kids. And Lee always had time to help —that is, unless his wife was around. Olive Furdell never seemed to like the way Lee spent so much time helping other people.

Lee hadn't heard about Miss Thurgood's leaving yet, so Harry started off by telling him about that. Lee smiled about Miss Thurgood sitting in the water—he wasn't the kind to laugh right out loud very much—and he said he would keep his ears open when he went to the candy store supply place that afternoon and see if he could hear of anyone who was looking for a good place to board.

Then Harry led into his main reason for coming. You'd think it would be hard to explain something as personal as trying to get your mother to marry somebody, but it really wasn't. You could tell Lee almost anything without feeling embarrassed.

"That's a funny thing," Lee said, when he finished.

44

"The very same possibility occurred to me some time ago. I liked Hal Brighton the first time I met him, and not long ago I was thinking that it would be a fine thing if he and Lorna Marco took a notion to get married. Running that big bording house *is* too hard a job for a woman all by herself, just as you say. And I'm inclined to think that you've picked a fine husband and father prospect. But you say you haven't noticed any symptoms that they're thinking along the same lines?"

"No," Harry said, "they like each other all right, you can tell that. But just friendly, you know."

Mr. Furdell sighed. "It's quite a problem," he said. "As a rule, it's a bit hard for a third party to influence these things, one way or the other. But there must be something you can do. I'm going to give it some careful thought."

Just then Olive Furdell called from inside the house, "Leland! Leland!" Her voice always went up high and screechy on the second syllable. Lee went back to the clothesline, and Harry headed for the alley.

"I'll think about it," Lee called over his shoulder, his voice coming out mumbly around the clothespin in his mouth. "I'll let you know if I think of anything."

Harry was halfway down the alley when Mrs. Furdell came out onto the back porch, but he heard every word she said. You had to be farther away than that to get out of earshot of Olive Furdell. "Leland, I swear to goodness, you're the slowest man alive. Are you going to take all day to hang up that little dab of wash?"

As far as Harry could tell, Lee didn't say anything at all. Harry took a hard kick at a little pebble on the

45

sidewalk, sighed, and went on down the alley.

He didn't get another chance to talk to Lee that day. And even though he did a lot of thinking about it, he didn't come up with any good ideas for the Plan. That night, when he was helping Mom in the kitchen, he decided to bring up the subject of Mr. Brighton to see if he could find out just what Mom really thought about him. But he'd just gotten the conversation going, when the door bell rang.

When Harry opened the front door, there on the dimly lit veranda, stood Mr. Tarzack Mazzeeck. He was looking every bit as round and wrinkled and unreal as he had the day before. "Dear me," he said, "I do hope you still have a vacancy. One that I could have for three or four days."

# Mr. Mazzeeck

Harry was really surprised when he opened the front door and found Mr. Mazzeeck standing there. He'd almost forgotten about him. Of course he had intended to tell Mom all about the suitcase and jumping off the bus and everything, but with all the excitement about Miss Thurgood, he'd just never gotten around to it. Actually he had remembered for a minute when Mom was being so worried over the money; but he'd decided it wasn't worth mentioning. For one thing, Mr. Mazzeeck had said he was a traveling salesman, so there wasn't any chance he'd be a permanent guest. And besides there had been a pretty good chance that he wouldn't show up at all.

But now, here he was on the doorstep, with the same great big suitcase and another smaller one. "Sure, Mr. Mazzeeck," Harry said, "we have a swell room for you. Come on in and sit down and I'll tell my mom you're here."

When Harry and Mom came back from the kitchen, Mr. Mazzeeck was perched on the edge of a chair hugging his big suitcase on his lap, just as he'd done on the bus bench. The little suitcase was on the floor by his feet. Harry introduced him to Mom, and Mom told him all the things he had to know about hours for meals, and being called in the morning. Then she got out the register for him to sign. He still had the suitcase on his lap and he tried to balance the registry on top of the suitcase to write his name. But he couldn't quite reach, and the whole thing kept wobbling around till the book got away from him and fell on the floor. So he finally put the suitcase down, but very carefully and right in front of his feet. Judging by his own past experience, Harry was pretty sure that it wasn't a very good place for it. Mr. Mazzeeck finished signing the book, stood up and, sure enough, he fell right over the suitcase. He probably would have gone smack on his face if Harry hadn't grabbed his arm. After he got his balance again he thanked Harry all over the place, but a second later, when Harry tried to pick up the suitcase to carry it upstairs for him, he jerked it away.

"No, no," he said. "I will carry that one. You may bring the other, if you please." And he started off up the stairs.

Harry looked back over his shoulder at Mom and grinned, and she grinned back and raised an eyebrow. Harry knew that she meant, "That's a strange one."

Mr. Mazzeeck was strange all right, you had to admit that. Strange and funny and sort of mysterious, too. But Harry couldn't help liking him. There was something about him that made Harry feel good. For one thing, it was easy to see that they had some things in common—like a handful of thumbs and two left feet.

In the next couple of days Harry didn't see much of Mr. Mazzeeck. Not that Harry was too busy with other things, or anything like that. As a matter of fact, he was around most of the time. He read a little, talked over the back fence to Lee once or twice, and worked some on his Plan, when he could think of something to do on it, anyway.

He did manage once to get Mom and Mr. Brighton out on the veranda together, one night after dinner. They didn't stay very long, but Harry was encouraged anyway. It was a typical summer night in San Francisco, and to stay outdoors at all without a coat, you'd have to be feeling pretty romantic.

Harry didn't see Mr. Mazzeeck just because he wasn't around the house very much. He went out in the morning with his big suitcase, and he didn't come back until almost dinner time. He didn't talk much at the table even when the other boarders asked him questions. He ate a lot, though, and Harry noticed he really did seem to enjoy the food—particularly Mom's good desserts.

It was because of noticing about the desserts that Harry happened to go into Mr. Mazzeeck's room. On the third night after his arrival at Marco's, Mr. Mazzeeck came back from wherever he went every day, too late for dinner. Mom and Harry were both in the living room when he came in, carrying his big suitcase and looking more tired and worried than ever.

"I was most distressed over missing one of your wonderful dinners, Mrs. Marco," he said, "but I was detained by a customer."

"Would you like to come out in the kitchen and let me warm something up for you?" Mom said. Mom must have thought that he looked pitiful, too, because she didn't usually do that sort of thing. If a boarder was late for dinner, it was just too bad for him. Mom had enough to do without cooking and washing dishes all over again.

"Oh, that is most kind of you, but no thank you. I wouldn't think of letting you go to so much trouble. Besides, I had a bite to eat at a restaurant."

But it seemed to Harry that he looked a bit wistful. It was that wistful look mostly, but also just plain curiosity, that sent Harry up to Mr. Mazzeeck's room a little later. You couldn't help wondering about such a strange little man with such a mysterious big suitcase. And there *had* been some pineapple upside-down cake left over from dinner.

So, at about eight o'clock, Harry knocked at the door of Mr. Mazzeeck's room with two pieces of cake and a cup of coffee on a tray. The door opened a little way, and Mr. Mazzeeck put his head out. He was wearing a sort of bathrobe thing with long flowing sleeves. It was dark purple with squiggly red figures all over it. When he saw the cake, his startled look changed to a smile—a hungry smile. He said, "My, my, doesn't that look delicious. How very thoughtful of you." He opened the door wide enough to let Harry in.

"Mom said I could have a bed-time snack," Harry said. "I thought you might like to keep me company. It's terrific cake."

"Quite so, quite so, I am delighted. Won't you sit

down." Mr. Mazzeeck got them both chairs, and when
they had started in on the cake he said, "You are, indeed, a most unusual young person. Let me see, you
said your name was Harry?"

"That's right, Harry Houdini Marco. My dad named me that. He was a magician, and he was crazy about Harry Houdini."

"Harry Houdini Marco? And the son of a magician. How remarkable. How extraordinarily remarkable." Mr. Mazzeeck stopped eating with a forkful of cake halfway to his mouth. Most people were interested or amused when Harry told them his full name, but Mr. Mazzeeck seemed absolutely flabbergasted. Harry was beginning to get a little uncomfortable when the man finally stopped staring and asked, "I suppose you have begun your training?"

"Training?"

"Yes, your apprenticeship. With whom are you studying the art of magic?"

"Oh, to be a magician, you mean. No, I'm not studying with anybody."

"Ah, that is a shame. You must begin soon now. The good ones all begin very young."

Harry had been getting ready to say that he just wasn't the magician type, but Mr. Mazzeeck sounded so enthusiastic that it seemed a shame to disappoint him. So he only said, "I guess you're right about that. My dad started practicing magic when he was just a little kid. He used to tell me about it. Are you a magician, too?"

"No, no," Mr. Mazzeeck said. "I am a salesman. I am only a traveling salesman, but at one time I was . . . I was something more than that." His voice trailed off into a sigh. For an uncomfortably long time he said nothing at all. Harry looked at him curiously, but Mr.

52

Mazzeeck didn't seem to notice. He looked different somehow, as he had that time before; his eyes were dark and hollow with remembering, as if they were looking backwards to a far, far past.

He began to say something, but not exactly to Harry. "So many years, so many changes . . ." he muttered. "Even magic changes . . . Most of it mere trickery now, mumbo-jumbo . . . Grand old dreams all forgotten . . . Nobody has the time and space any more . . ."

As Harry watched, wondering, he suddenly had a split-second impression, so strange and spooky that it made a shiver zig-zag up his spine. It was as if, for just a moment, Mr. Mazzeeck's funny chubby face had turned into a transparent mask, and from beneath it another face looked through. Another face, older and yet ageless, with eyes that burned with a deep dark power.

It was just a glimpse, and then Mr. Mazzeeck looked like himself again and his eyes seemed to come back into focus. "Take boys, for instance," he said, in an accusing tone of voice. "Do they dream of wielding Excalibur or taming Pegasus?" He shook his finger in Harry's face. "Or do your dreams rise no higher than a baseball bat or a bicycle?"

"Gee, Mr. Mazzeeck," Harry said. "I don't dream about things like that. I would like to have a new tenspeed, but I don't *dream* about it." He had been feeling pretty uneasy, and now he felt a little guilty, too, without really knowing why.

But just then Mr. Mazzeeck calmed down to his usual sort of nervous embarrassment. "I'm so sorry," he said. "I'm afraid I've been taking out my problems on you, and of course, you are entirely blameless. You must forgive me, but my business has not been going well lately, and I am very tired."

He stood up suddenly and put his empty plate back on the tray. "The cake was most delicious, and I find myself even more deeply indebted to you. You must visit me again, sometime."

Harry knew an invitation to leave when he heard one, but when he turned to pick up the tray, he noticed something that stopped him in his tracks. On the foot of the bed, with its top wide open, sat the mysterious suitcase. He took a step or two backwards; but almost as quickly, Mr. Mazzeeck must have realized what he was trying to do. He had time for only a tiny glimpse of the contents of the suitcase before Mr. Mazzeeck had stepped in front of it, hiding it from view.

Afterwards, Harry didn't quite remember what he'd said next or just how he'd said good-by. He had a general impression that they'd both been very polite and that Mr. Mazzeeck had asked him to come again. But it wasn't surprising that Harry's mind had been on something else, at the time. In fact, his mind was on that something else for a long, long time. It wasn't the kind of thing you could just forget about. You don't just forget that there is a strange man living in your own house who carries in his suitcase a long, sharp, evil-looking sword.

# The Sword
# and Other Problems

That night, Harry lay awake for hours, wondering and worrying. He didn't want to tell Mom and get her all worried, too, unless there really was a reason. And maybe there wasn't any reason. Maybe there was a perfectly understandable explanation of why a strange-acting little man should be sneaky and suspicious about his suitcase and why it should contain, among other strange-looking objects, a long, sharp, gleaming sword. The trouble was, it was pretty hard for Harry to imagine what that explanation could be.

He might be a professional sword swallower, for instance, except that wouldn't explain why he pretended to be a salesman, and why he was so secretive. There's no reason to pretend you're not a sword swallower if you are one.

Still, in spite of its weaknesses, that was just about the best possibility that Harry could come up with. Possibility! There was that word again! It was beginning to look as if the Swami were right and the air really was full of possibilities. Only right now, some of them were almost too awful to think about. Like, for instance, the fact that a boarding house might be a good place to hide in if you'd committed some terrible deed; the kind of deed you might do with a big—sword.

The worst of it was that if something terrible did happen, it would be Harry's fault. After all, he was the one who had asked Mr. Mazzeeck to come to the boarding house.

After lying awake half the night, Harry finally decided the best thing to do would be to keep quiet, for the time being, and just try to keep an eye on Mr. Mazzeeck. It wouldn't be for long. Mr. Mazzeeck had already been at Marco's for three days and he'd said something about three or four days when he arrived. Besides, it was very unusual for a traveling salesman to stay more than a few days at a time. But, of course, that sort of depended on whether Mr. Mazzeeck really was a traveling salesman.

It wasn't four days, or five, or even six. Mr. Mazzeeck was right there at Marco's for a whole week after that night when Harry first saw the sword. And during that week all sorts of terrible things happened. Not that Mr. Mazzeeck murdered anyone in his sleep or did any of the other awful things Harry had imagined. What did happen, were things that had never even occurred to him.

In the first place, it was the very next day that Clarissa Clyde came to stay at Marco's Boarding House. When Mom called Harry into the living room to carry Miss Clyde's bright red imitation alligator luggage upstairs, he didn't realize that more trouble had arrived. In fact, he was feeling pretty happy that they had a new boarder, who might be permanent. It was somebody to take Miss Thurgood's place—and someone who might be a little more interesting, too.

For one thing, Miss Clyde was a night club singer. He'd overheard her telling Mom so. That was something new and different for Marco's. As far as Harry could remember, they'd never had any kind of singer before. And even if Miss Clyde was strange looking, at least she was a change from Miss Thurgood.

Miss Clyde was a big woman, not fat exactly, but a good bit wider than Mom, at least in places. She was probably as old as Mom, but it was a little hard to tell because her real face was all cluttered over with make-up. Her hair was a stiff yellow color, like a doll in a store window, and her red and white dress looked as if it wasn't quite big enough to fit her.

But the happiness about having a new boarder didn't last very long; at least not for Harry. Right away, he found out one awful thing: she called people Sweetie. Everybody—even boys. When Harry got to the top of the stairs with her luggage, she gave him a dime and said, "There you go, Sweetie. Thanks a million."

That was bad enough, but something worse started happening that night at dinner. It began almost the very moment Mom introduced Miss Clyde to the rest of the boarders. Right away Miss Clyde popped herself down next to Mr. Brighton, and even before the very first meal was over she was calling him "Sweetie" and "Hal" and flopping her long sticky-looking eyelashes up and down.

Harry was really disgusted. He saw what she was

doing right away. It was just like when Miss Dutton started in on the beauty shop man, only about a million times worse. It was all so obvious you couldn't help noticing, but Mom didn't seem to. At least, she didn't fight back at all, like flopping her eyelashes, too, and giggling, or any of the other things women do when they want somebody's attention. Harry did the best he could by trying to start a conversation with Mr. Brighton about the Giants' shut-out game against the Dodgers. But Mr. Brighton didn't seem to be in the mood for baseball. It was a terrible meal.

By that evening Harry had decided that there wasn't anything he could do about Clarissa Clyde, at least not right then; but it was that very night that he thought of something he could do about Mr. Mazzeeck. Or, at least, something that might help him find out what the guy was up to. The thing that occurred to him was that there was a way to look in the window of Mr. Mazzeeck's room.

The old carriage house on the Furdell place was right next to the edge of Marco's property. It was a huge old barn-like place with all sorts of curly wood-trimmings. It had a slanted roof and above that a little flat one, like a platform, with a railing around it. There were stairs that led up to the flat roof on the outside of the building. Mr. Furdell said that his grandfather used to be a ship's captain, and he had had it built that way so he could watch the ships on the bay.

Anyway, there was a swell view from up there, and if you looked towards the west you could look right into the second-story windows of the two old houses.

Harry waited until it was good and dark before he slipped through the gate to the Furdell's yard and up the stairs to the roof of the carriage house. Just as he had hoped, the blind was up in Mr. Mazzeeck's room and the light was on. Harry could clearly see the picture of a vase of roses and an apple on the opposite side of the room, but for a long time he didn't see anything of Mr. Mazzeeck. If he was in the room he certainly wasn't moving around much.

It seemed like more than an hour that Harry knelt behind the railing and peered into Mr. Mazzeeck's room. At least it was long enough for him to get awfully cold and damp and stiff. Then, just as he made up his mind to give up, he saw Mr. Mazzeeck walk across the room.

Harry sat back down with a thump. A few seconds later, Mr. Mazzeeck came back across the room looking at something in his hands. He crossed the room to the window and glanced out. Harry caught just a glimpse of the thing in his hands—something golden and shiny—before Mr. Mazzeeck pulled down the blind.

But at that point Mr. Mazzeeck made a mistake. He didn't seem to realize that even though the shade was down, the window could still be dangerous. It didn't seem to occur to him that if he really didn't want to be seen, he shouldn't stand so near a thin window-shade with a light on behind him.

Immediately there appeared on the window-shade a short, well-rounded silhouette, as clear and sharp as the figures in a magic lantern show. It was unmistakably Mr. Mazzeeck, and he appeared to be doing something

60